欢迎加入后浪读书俱乐部 www.hinabook.com

- 加入我们,可以得到定期的新书信息、电子读书报、活动信息、后浪小礼物、购书优惠券、作者签名书籍和海报、毛边书等等。
- 俱乐部将从每月新增会员中抽取 3 名赠送当月最新出版的书籍一本。
- 会员书评投稿如获纸媒发表将有机会获得后浪新书 1 本。
- 欢迎登陆 http://www.hinabook.com 和 www.pmovie.com 了解更多活动信息。

*本活动最终解释权归后浪出版咨询(北京)有限责任公司所有

个人资料（请务必完整填写并回传）

姓名 _____ □先生/□女士

Email _____ 生日_____年___月___日

固定电话 _____ - _____ 手机 _____

单位 _____ 职业 _____

地址 _____

_____

QQ/MSN _____ 邮编 _____

读者调查表

您从哪本书得到这张卡片的？_____

您从哪里购得本书的？_____

您的阅读方向？_____

_____

您还希望我们出版或引进哪类书？_____

_____

您的意见或建议？_____

_____

如何加入后浪读书俱乐部？

1. 拨打热线010-57499090，向客服人员登记您的信息。
2. 发短信至18811421266，我们将回电登记您的信息。
3. 将此信息登记表传真至：010-64018116
4. 登陆网站：www.hinabook.com，点击右上角"注册"，填写会员信息登记表。
5. 邮寄至：北京市东城区景山东街纳福胡同13号北楼2层 后浪出版咨询（北京）有限责任公司 邮编：100009

后浪微信：hinabook

后浪官方直营店 http://bjhlts.tmall.com
服务邮箱 buy@hinabook.com
服务电话 13366573072　010-57499090

后浪出版公司

The Rubáiyát of Omar Khayyám

Omar Khayyám

鲁拜集

［波斯］奥玛·海亚姆 著
［英］爱德华·菲茨吉拉德 等 英译
鹤西 中译
苏利文 版画插图

程侃声（笔名鹤西，1908—1999）

中译者简介

程侃声(1908—1999),原名铎声,字信川,笔名鹤西,中国水稻种质资源学家,文学家,翻译家。其祖父程健斋(1851—1928),名道恒,字健斋,自号绀泉饮者,诗人、语言学家,著有《绀泉饮者诗抄》、《安陆方言考》等著作。其父亲程逸滨(1885—1945),名家颖,是中国同盟会会员、著名法学家、音韵学家,1903年留学日本早稻田大学,主修政治经济,著有《日本登记制度调查报告书》、《台湾土地制度考察报告》等。

程侃声生于湖北安陆市曹家冲（现安陆市白兆村）。他10岁前在家读私塾,10岁后随父到北平,先后就读于北平高等师范学堂附小和附中(现和平门外北京师范大学附小、附中)。在北平就读的几年,他深受"五四"新文学运动的影响,经常在《晨报诗刊》、《小说月报》、《华北日报》、《新中华日报》上发表诗文和译稿,同杨晦、塞先艾、废名、冯至、张骏祥等成为文笔挚友,也曾得到叶圣陶先生的赏识与鼓励。

1927年,程侃声以第一名的成绩考入北平大学农学院。1931年毕业后,在广西、湖北、云南等地从事棉花、黄麻、烟草、甘蔗和花生等经济作物的研究。解放后在云南从事水稻研究,提出"三性(即感光性、感温性、短日高温生育期)重组"的杂交水稻观点;提出亚洲栽培稻的分类体系,首创"形态指数法"鉴别籼稻和粳稻。程侃声一生从事农业科学研究工作60余年,对我国稻种资源的搜集整理、分类、起源演化等方面的研究作出了突出的贡献,为水稻的杂交育种研究做出了奠基性工作。其晚年汇总的毕生的研究成果《论栽培植物的生态分类》,被吴征镒院士评介为

"其成就绝不比金善宝院士之于小麦、丁颖院士之于华南籼稻(逊色),也不逊色于吴觉农先生之于茶,章文才先生之于柑橘。"他工作上诚笃敬业、严谨治学、精益求精,学术上从不盲从附合,曲意逢迎;程侃声做人胸襟坦荡,待人真诚,操守清廉,无论在治学上或是在为人方面都堪称一代风范,人之楷模。

1978年,程侃声主持的云南稻种资源研究获全国科学大会奖;1981年他和中国农业科学院共同主持的云南稻种资源考察获农业部农牧渔业重要科技成果一等奖;1982年水稻新品种"云粳136"获云南省科技成果三等奖;1985年"云南省稻种资源的综合研究与利用"项目通过部级鉴定获云南省科技成果一等奖;1986年担任中国作物遗传资源研究委员会(后改为中国作物遗传资源学会)第一届主任(理事长);1990年起作为第一批享受国务院颁发的政府特殊津贴的科学家。程侃声先后担任过云南省农业科学院院长和名誉院长、云南省人大代表和常委、云南省科协副主席、云南省农学会副理事长等职务,有《亚洲稻籼粳亚种的鉴别》、《亚洲稻的起源与演化——活物的考古》、《程侃声稻作论文选集》等存世。

20世纪90年代中期,程侃声从农业研究第一线退休。他在闲暇时写下一系列追忆旧事的文章,1987年结集为《野花野菜集》,1997年出版《初冬的朝颜》等。2003年后人结集出版《鹤西文集》。

目　录

菲茨吉拉德和海亚姆的《鲁拜集》（代序） ... 1

《鲁拜集》选译 ... 1

译后记 ... 153

RUBÁIYÁT OF OMAR KHAYYÁM (FIFTH VERSION) ... 155
 OMAR KHAYYÁM —— THE ASTRONOMER-POET OF PERSIA ... 157
 RUBÁIYÁT OF OMAR KHAYYÁM ... 171

出版后记 ... 197

菲茨吉拉德和海亚姆的《鲁拜集》

（代序）　小泉八云

爱德华·菲茨吉拉德（Edward Fitzgerald）生于1809年，就学于剑桥大学。在剑桥他结识了丁尼生和其他许多文坛上的著名人物。他继承了大量遗产，使他不从事什么职业也能毕生研究文学和艺术。他住在乡下一栋舒适的房屋里，拥有各种语言的书籍，很少在社会上露面。他最初印行的作品只是为了给朋友们看的——甚至在扉页上都没有署上自己的名字。他活到很大的年纪，在死前不久才出了名。菲茨吉拉德的作品的美在开始并不为人们所理解，现在则被公认为伟大的名著。关于他本人也许只讲这些就可以了。但是关于他的著作还有一点要说明的是：它们并非原作——至少就通常的意义说是这样的。它们全都是西班牙文、波斯文和希腊文的翻译作品。这样你们也许会奇怪,怎么光凭译作能获得文学上最高的地位和荣誉呢?唯一可能的回答是菲茨吉拉德也许是世界上最好的翻译家。他不是直译,他译的是神韵、诗文的精髓。正是由于这一原因,他取得了前所未有的成就,甚至在未来几百年中可能也无人能够做到。他不仅有丰富的学识,也有精致的鉴赏力,在这一点上他使我们想到诗人格雷(Gray),他的生活和格雷也有颇多相似之处。

  菲茨吉拉德翻译的奥玛·海亚姆(Omar Khayyám)的四行诗集是一部杰作。奥玛·海亚姆是一位十一世纪后半叶的波斯诗人。他的故事是很有趣也很特殊的。十一世纪时在波斯一个叫乃沙堡(今伊朗的内沙布尔——译者)的城中,有三个学生在一个不大的学校里跟一位著名的教师学习回教的经典。这三人结成了深厚的友谊,并在有一天达成了这样的协议——就是不管三人中哪一个最先取得了成就,他就要在力所能及的范围内尽量地帮助其他两人。其中一个学生就是著名的尼赞·乌尔·穆洛克(Nizám-ul-Mulk),他后来做了阿尔普·阿斯兰苏丹(Sultán Alp Arslan)的首相;第二个学生就是我们的诗人奥玛·海亚姆(Omar Khayyám);第三个叫霍山·本·萨巴(Hasan Ben Sabbáh),他后来成为世界历史上一个最恐怖的名字。那时候三个人都还是少年,但是他们知道这个学校里的高材生一般都会得到好的位置,所以他们一起做出这个友谊的协定。几年过后,一个青年真的做了首相。于是他的老朋友霍山来找他,得到了在政府中的一个职位。随后奥玛·海亚姆也来了。他和首相说："我不要什么高的职位和荣誉，只请你给我一份不大的年金，使我能将我的一生贡献于诗歌和研究。"于是首相给了他一份优厚的年金和一所皇宫旁的小房屋，他就住在那里一直到死。对于他给予奥玛的善意，首相是毫无遗憾的。但是霍山的情况就完全不同了。霍山对他的恩人和旧友图谋不轨，很快被发现并被驱逐出国。后来霍山在叙利亚建立了一个从未有过的恐怖团体——这就是被称为伊斯迈里教派（Ismailians）或者回教暗杀徒（Assassins）的暗杀团。你们也许在东方史上读到过他们。他们有一条规矩，就是当首领叫一个人去刺杀一位王子或国王时，刺客就必须遵命前往。这个秘密团体曾刺杀过许多国王和王子；暗杀团使用的武器是有毒的。你们也许记得英国的爱德华皇帝就曾被他们的人刺伤过，只是由于他的妻子英勇地从伤口中吸出了毒液才救活了他。刺客们的首领就是这个举世闻名的"山中老人"；霍山和他的伙伴们住在几乎上不去的山岩里边，所以这个团体一直存在到鞑靼人入侵后才被消灭。可是远在被消灭之前，霍山就派人把他的老朋友、首相尼赞刺杀了。

不过奥玛一直受到宫廷的眷爱，始终住在他的小房子里写着关于人生、爱情、酒和玫瑰的诗歌（同时，他也是当时著名的数学家和天文学家——译者）。因为他对那时代的宗教狂热毫无同情，他曾被许多人看作是一位非常渎神而不敬的诗人；但他似乎受到了宫廷中朋友们的保护。我想你们都知道回教教义是严格禁酒的，在一切事情上都很严肃,要求过极简单的生活。这一教导在最初是很好的,早期的哈里发们也是很严格遵守的。他们知道伊斯兰教的许多大的战争都是来自沙漠的阿拉伯骑兵打赢的,这些骑兵们具有自我牺牲和吃苦精神,可以每天只吃一顿简单的食物。但是后来这教义被一些狂热团体推向了极端,最后使得一方面是超过常情的禁欲主义,另一方面却是毫无节制的奢侈。禁欲主义的宗教诗歌在奥玛的时代还处在上升时期。这种禁欲主义宗教因素,有的地方非常像印度的宗教,或者说,很可能受到了印度哲学的影响。在回教中还有一种神秘主义,相信经过严格的修炼可以获得神奇的智慧。他们相信人和神圣的宇宙是统一的。他们还相信许许多多奇怪的事情,并且创立了不同的宗派,彼此间不断地争辩。也许就是对这一切的蔑视,使奥玛·海亚姆写出了他的著名的诗歌。他大胆地采取了这一立场,认为我们不知道也不可能知道来世的一切,或者什么超自然的世界。他宣扬我们所知道的一切就是这个感知的世界,人们最好是从现实生活中尽可能正当地获得快乐,而不要去考虑宇宙的神秘。他的诗作的伟大而不朽的魅力则在于他处理叫我们不要去为宇宙操劳这一问题的方式。生命的无常,死亡之谜,青春的凋逝,要解释不能解释的事是愚蠢的哲学尝试,等等 —— 这些就是奥玛·海亚姆在他的最引人和最美的诗中带着哀愁和嘲弄的幽默所表达的。

菲茨吉拉德这位英译者精确地再现了这些四行诗的东方韵律 —— 它在四行中,除了第三行以外都是押韵的。(偶尔也有四行都有韵的,但这是一种例外。)对这种东方韵律的模拟给英国文学带来了一种全新的诗的形式。

现在让我们回到诗文上,看几首奥玛叹息生命无常的四行诗。他先问,什么是生命?它不过是在无尽的旅程中一个暂时的休息之地。在这点上他的想法和佛教箴言中说的"生命是在路旁旅店里暂时的停留"非常相似。这是个东方式的意象。

>这帐篷只是供他一夜的休歇,
>苏丹啊也正被带往死亡的陵穴;
>苏丹起床了,侍者铺平床单,
>准备迎送另一位过客。

侍者(Ferrash)每晚为旅客准备好帐篷并在清晨铺平被褥。海亚姆又把生命比作一个旅行队在沙漠井泉边一瞬的停留:

>一瞬的停留 —— 从沙漠中的井边
>匆匆喝一口生命的流泉 ——
>看呀!那幻影般的旅队已经走到了
>它所从来的虚空边缘
>　　　—— 寻乐莫迟延!

>你要是把一闪的生命用来探索
>人生的奥秘 —— 朋友,当心啊!
>真与伪也许只间隔一根头发,
>请告诉我,生命还凭借什么?

真与伪也许只间隔一根头发;
是啊,也许就只是那一字之差——
要是你真能发现它

　　　　　——你也许就找到了天堂
或者还有那作为万物之主的**他**;

他的神秘的存在,在造物的川流中
像水银一样流动,使你徒劳追踪,
他会化作各样的形体,如鱼似月,
这也都将改变和死亡

　　　　　——而**他**却无始无终。

  他说,生命只不过是旅行人在沙漠的绿洲上停一会儿来喝点水。沙漠就是我们不知道的无垠;我们停留的生命之井就是这个世界,我们是从神秘中来,向虚无而去。我们喝点水又走,最后消失在我们所从来的虚无之中。在不可测的神秘的黑暗里,一个人的生命只不过是一点小小的闪光——像一块金属片上的闪光,我们要去探索事物的秘密有什么用呢?秘密是无限的,而我们是短暂的;为什么要把这一瞬浪费来寻找我们找不出的东西?你说,我们要发现真理;可谁知道真理是什么?很可能真与伪的距离还不到一根头发丝宽,或者只是一个字母的差异,如果你能找出这点点的差异来,那么你也就可能发现你到了天堂,或者站在制造这一切秘密的至高无上的存在(Supreme Being)之前了。但是你不可能找得出这些差异的。对于他,你此生此世是什么也不会知道的。他无所不在,每样东西中都有他,但是你却抓不到他,正像你抓不起一滴水银一样。只有一件事可以肯定:他就是一切有形之物,从地上的鱼到天上的月亮,并且一切形体都会死亡和消逝——虽然他自己是永远也不会变的。

我们很惊奇地发现最后这首诗的思想非常近于印度哲学。此外我们还看到更多的奇似之处:一位古代的梵文诗人曾把看到的世界比作一局象棋,是神自己和自己下得好玩的。奥玛也几乎毫不走样地表现了同一印象。神,他告诉我们,是看不见的——只可猜测:

> 好像被猜到了——却又在帷幕后边,
> 围浸在黑暗中的戏还在上演,
> 这只是为了给**永恒**消遣
> **他**自己编剧,自己导演,又自己看。

好像是一场木偶戏——也是印度的比喻;而下面这些句子则更为动人——

> 我们不过是这样的一群
> 像走马灯似的往来的阴影,
> 围着太阳点着的灯笼在转,
> 半夜里高举这灯笼的是剧场的**主人**。

> 在这白天和黑夜交织的棋盘里,
> **他**拿这些无能为力的棋子游戏,
> 把他们这里那里挪动,又将军,又杀子,
> 最后啊一个个放回棋盒里歇息。

我们认为其中的第一首是所有的四行诗中最壮丽的。太阳被比作一个神奇的灯笼里的蜡烛,使得宇宙的各种影子显现在我们眼前,而我们自己也正是这些影子。此外则上上下下都是深夜中无穷的黑暗和无穷的神秘。神好像是打灯笼的人:因为在暗室中一幕幕演着的影戏,由于光和影的移动,我们才确知有演者的存在。还有其他的比喻也是非常美的,比如把时间看成是一个大的棋盘,黑的地方是黑夜,白的地方是白天(指国际象棋盘——译者)。

既然把我们只看作不可知的神所玩的棋子,诗人自然就会问,你何必还去管它,体会有什么遭遇呢?你能阻挡你的命运吗?当然不行。那又何必烦恼呢?你是像一个球,球不会问打球的人为什么打它,为什么要把它投向这边而不是那边。

    球啊,它无法问明这样或者那样
    而是由击球者打向左方右方;
    只有将你投入场地的**他**
    才知道这一切
      —— **他**才知详 —— **他**才知详!

这里的球场当然就是指的人生场地,而你是神打着玩的球。你对命运是莫可奈何的;祈祷也没有用处。

    那动着的手指在写,写过了又写下去,
    不管你有多么聪明,有怎样虔诚的情绪,
    都不会唤回**他**删去半行,
    所有你的泪水也不会洗掉它一字一句。

东方人对于命运的神圣之感再没有比在上面的诗句中表现得更为壮丽的了。但是怎样看待宗教上关于地狱与天堂，关于来世的善报和惩处之类的启示呢？对这些对象，诗人公开地表示他是一点也不相信的。来世吗？哪个死去的人曾回来过？能说得出一点消息？所有关于这些事情写下的书都只是胡言乱语——像诗人说的，谎言。

哦，对地狱的恐惧，对天堂的希望！
至少一件事还是真的
　　　　——此生正在飞翔，
只有这件事是真的，其他都是说谎；
曾经开放的花儿已永远凋亡。

这岂不奇怪？成千上万的人
在我们之前走进了那黑暗的门，
却没有一个回来告诉我们，
哪里是我们要去的途程。

圣徒和学者给过我们很多教导，
他们生在我们之前，已被当作先知埋掉，
都不过是一些梦话，是他们从睡梦中醒来
告诉旁人的，跟着又睡他们的长觉。

我叫我的灵魂去那虚无之乡，
对身后的情况进行探访；
慢慢地他又回到我的身边，
回复说："我自己就是地狱，也是天堂。"

> 天堂不过是欲望得到满足的幻景,
> 地狱是一个煎熬中灵魂的暗影,
> 投身在这黑暗之中,从那里我们
> 出来是如此之晚,而归去又过早地凋零。

我们有一则格言说,天堂和地狱就在你心中。我们的格言与这则古代的波斯诗篇的相似实在是让人惊奇的。奥玛还叙述了他自己追求真理的历史:他明显地嘲笑说 —— 在他看来,所有的哲学家都是骗子,所有的教义都是胡言。

> 所有圣哲和智者关于两个世界的谈话,
> 不管它们是怎样的浩瀚无涯,
> 都不过是愚蠢的预言。他们的话
> 一钱不值,他们的嘴也塞满了泥巴。
>
> 当我年青的时候,我曾带着渴望去访问
> 博士和圣人,听那些伟大的高论
> 说天堂和地狱是这样或者那样,
> 而每次出来时却还是当初我进去的门。
>
> 我们一起播智慧的种,
> 我还亲手让它生长茏葱;
> 可是我只有这点儿收获啊 ——
> 我是来如流水去如风。
>
> 不知道是为了什么,来到这宇宙中间,
> 不知道从何而来,像流水潺潺,

> 离开这世界,像沙漠里的风,
> 呜呜地吹着,也不知去向哪边。

据说尼赞·乌尔·穆洛克首相在被暗杀者刺伤而濒死的时候,念诵的就是最后这首诗。宇宙的一切问题都说在里边了。这确是一种不可知的处境,但我们将会看到,它和相信无限之力(Infinite)不是不可调和的。他告诉我们,没有一个人类的心灵能够回答为什么、哪里来、哪里去这三个问题,对这一秘密的研究也都是徒劳的。海亚姆曾刻苦学习过,但是他发现,在这世界上他只是像水一样来,像风一样离去。关于他的学习,他告诉我们的还不只这些。海亚姆不愿让我们以为他缺乏信仰是出于无知。他研究过所有各派的哲学和当时的一些科学 —— 天文学和数学。像研究宗教著作一样,他也研究过自然这本书,但他找不到答案;永恒的神秘依然存在着。

> 经过第七道门我从地心上来,
> 在七重天顶的宝座上入座,
> 看见路两旁许多结儿都已解开,
> 只有人类命运的主结依然还在。

> 这里是我找不到钥匙的门户;
> 这里是我看透不了的帷幕;
> 这帷幕这边谈到**我**和**你**
> 一会儿,**你**和**我**就永远湮没。

> **你**让我活动，却躲在帷幕后边，
> 我伸手想看看黑暗里是否有明灯一盏；
> 从外边好像听到一个声音在喊——
> 你身中的**我**什么也看不见。

这些概念在一个普通的英国读者看来也许是奇特的，但我想它们对你们这些研究过东方哲学的学生一定不陌生。奥玛是想用少量的字说出他的研究过程，关于"我和你"的谈论其实是关于灵魂问题的讨论：我们每个人是不同于无限的个体，还是和它是一体的？有些人说他有主观和客观的存在，有些人以同样有力的论证说是没有。有人宣扬有个性，别人又告诉他无所谓个性，一切有情之物只是一个无限存在的表现。他准备不再去想自己身中的无限，忽然他好像听到一个喊声说："你身中的我什么也看不见。"这不是非常接近佛教所说的，我们体内的灵魂，在我们超越现世的不满的存在之前是不能观不能觉的教义吗？但这也一定会使西方读者想起叔本华的一个奇怪而有力的比喻来。叔本华说过人类的意识不能看见自己——我们的视神经对自己仿佛是瞎的一样。

人类想解开宇宙之谜的一切努力都毫无用处。诗人于是说："让我们至少理智地如实地看待这个世界，接受自然给我们的美和爱和快乐而不要枉费心机地去思考我们永不会知道的事物吧。"

> 不要为天上人间的事陷入迷惘，
> 明日的麻烦最好是让它随风飘扬；

> 且把你的手指插入她的卷发，
> 莫辜负那苗条女郎的劝酒持觞。

"明日的麻烦"诗人指的是未来之谜；他说到的酒也不能一味只从字面的意义来理解。酒在回教立法中是严加禁止的，这里不仅是指的葡萄酒，而是一切感官的快乐 —— 人世的欢乐。在波斯人中间，现在都还常常把美丽的女郎比作柏树，因为柏树高而苗条。在波斯的宴会上常常叫女奴隶来给客人敬酒。在《天方夜谭》里，你们可以看到许多写这类宴会的文字，这些女郎常常是披着头发的。我们可以意译为："不要再为了什么是人间的、什么是神圣的这类题目为难，不要再去想那些来世的神秘；宴饮吧，也不要怕摸着那给你斟酒的美女的头发。"

> 假如你现在喝的酒和吻着的朱唇
> 都没入了万物生灭的永恒，
> 只消想今天你还是和昨天一样，
> 明天你也不会有损毫分。

显然美是在飞逝的，没有一样事是持久的，快乐很快就会过去，生命也是这样。当有人告诉你生命始于和终于乌有时，你就回答他，正因为如此，你现在不过是你过去的样子，在将来你也不会有所增减。这个逻辑中有一点冷嘲的味道。假如一切都是幻境的话，那么我们喜欢或不喜欢这个幻境还有什么差别呢？不管我们是愉快地接受它或者恐惧地躲避它，不管我们是道德高尚或者不然 —— 在万物永恒的秩序上又有什么关系？只为对来世的生活有疑虑而摒绝享乐，—— 这是多么愚蠢！否，把生命看作是一杯摆在你面前的酒；生命是让你高兴和快乐的，不是让你流泪、恐惧和怀疑的。喝下它，正如你在宴会上喝酒时一样；会享受生活的人，在日子来到的时候，也将能够更愉快地面对死亡。相信你一定不会比现在少什么的，将来你也不会比过去少。

> 假如死亡的天使在河边找到你，
> 把他的哑泉送到你的手里，
> 请你的灵魂来到唇边
> 一饮而尽 —— 你一点也莫犹疑。

死亡的天使就是无常(Azrael)；河边就是生命之河的尽头。还有一个更带着嘲弄，但却是很壮丽的比喻，它把人们的生命比作酒上的酒花 —— 我们是不是应该称之为宇宙的生命之酒呢？

> 不要怕有一天**生存**会合起你我的账本，
> 从此后一切就荡然无存；
> 那永生的**斟酒人**会从他的酒瓶里倒出
> 成百万我们这样的酒花，并不断酌斟。

原诗中的 Saki，可理解为宴会上侍酒的女郎或男童，这是一个大胆的比喻，但确是很美的 —— 神倾注着生命之酒，而它的酒花就是人类的灵魂。有酒就有酒花,而只要有生命存在,也就有苦与乐。生与死实际并不很重要,甚至也许差别不大;没有什么可喜或可怕的。在世上我们对自己对别人都要慷慨,像玫瑰一样。

> 看,我们周围的玫瑰正在盛开,
> 她说,"我笑着开向世界,
> 一下子我打开锦囊的丝缐,
> 向园里散尽我的资财。"

这里,玫瑰在说:"看我,瞧我是多么慷慨!我笑着到这世界上来,我一下子打开了我的荷包,把我所有的都散在地上。"这当然是指的很快凋落的芳香的花瓣。对于那些禁欲和纵欲的人们,其结果则是很相像的,一个人会从这方面或那方面变得愚蠢,过分的克制或者过分的放纵,任一极端都是糊涂;生命是一种宝贵的赠与,是我们应该享用的快乐。

> 有的人一颗颗收起那金色的谷粒,
> 有的人挥金如土,毫不爱惜,
> 他们都一样不会变成那贵重的黄金
> 一旦掩埋了,人们还想把它挖起。

意译是这样:那样小心地,像悭吝人一样,把生命的财富贮而不用的人,还有那些浪费它像浪子倾荡遗产的人 —— 他们的结果如何呢?他们都将化为地里的尘土;他们的灰烬彼此毫无区别,谁的尘土也不是黄金,不会再有人想去挖起他们。

> 人们倾心于尘世的希望,
> 有的成功了,有的只好埋葬,
> 像沙漠里的白雪,皑皑
> 一两个小时 —— 就不知去向。

这首诗的意思是说,不管抱负是成功还是失败,不管我们今天是幸运还是不幸运,结果都是一样的;万物都像沙漠中有时降下的雪,将在太阳的光热下立时消失。这的确不是一种安慰,我们不能不叹惋于事物的无常 ——

> 唉!那随着玫瑰凋谢而逝去的春光!
> 那中断了的青春而芬芳的篇章!
> 那在树枝中歌唱的夜莺,
> 谁知道是来自又去向何方!

这里提到了东方用麝香保存美丽的手稿的习惯,青春是被比作这样的篇章的 —— 诗人说,实在太快地就被捆置起来了;如果我们和神灵有机会将宇宙重新塑造一番的话,我们一定不让它像现在这个样子。

> 哦,我爱! 假如你和我能向**他**商量,
> 来掌握这可怜的万物的形象;
> 是不是我们要将它砸得粉碎,
> 把它塑造得更符合我们的愿望!

甚至园中的月亮的景象也使诗人感伤;他表现的

这种情绪,比过去一个日本诗人所写的还更深些。

> 那边又升起了照着我们的明月 ——
> 今后啊她还会不断地圆缺,
> 今后啊她还会升起来寻找我们,
> 但在这花园里 —— 有一人将遍寻不得。

这里是一个知道自己不久于人世的老人的叹息。但是使他至少还感到一点安慰的是他觉得他曾经享受了生活,喝了他能喝的酒。这里是他最后的遗愿,也是对侍酒人的祈求,对前边提到的苗条女郎的请求。

> 啊,女郎,几时你和她一样
> 在那草地上群星般的宾客中来往,
> 请你斟酒时把满满一杯美酒
> 倾洒在我曾经坐过的地方!

波斯诗人们也常常把美丽的妇女比作月亮 —— 特别是一弯新月。此诗的意译是:"美丽的女郎,当你在我死后的某个时候,走在坐在花园里的客人们中间,好像月亮经过群星一样,在你走到我坐过的地方时,请想到我,并把一杯酒倒在这里作为纪念。"

我所征引的这些可以说是代表了书中大部分著名的四行诗了。全书一共一百零一首。其中有些是逻辑性或者论辩式的,另外一些又有许多东方的典故,需要大量的说明,我就都没有引用了。不过我想你们已经可以知道这些诗歌的一般概念和诗人的主旨。还有个问题是他的哲学有什么价值？——或者我们能称之为一种哲学吗？从奥玛在八九个世纪以来一直在东方受到崇拜来看，它一定是还有某种价值的。甚至在今天的英国它也以一种奇异而可惊的方式使人们着迷。每年都有菲茨吉拉德译作的新版发行，这些版本从一美元到两百美元的都有（指二十世纪二十年代的价格——译者）。今年还出了诗集的集注本。对奥玛·海亚姆这种突然的风行，宗教界的人士是有些愤怒的，认为他是一个"大异教徒"——像丁尼生所称呼的。的确，从基督教的观点看，是大不敬的。但是实际上，对奥玛·海亚姆不必看得这么严重。我们应该把他看作一个优雅的诗人，他只是想说出对人生的一种看法，是和当时的狂热与伪善唱对台戏的。他宣传的是一种伊壁鸠鲁主义，一种泛神论——这两者在它们的范围内我们认为是完全正确的，但是都不是全部的真理。有一个故事可以说明这点，现在我就告诉你们。

我想你们都知道一个说明光和颜色的关系的科学试验，在一个或大或小的纸盒上涂上光谱中的不同颜色——红、黄、绿、蓝、紫。当圆转得很慢时，你能看到各种颜色。可是当圆盘转得极快时，色彩就消失了，圆盘变成了全白。提醒了这一点之后，现在就让我讲这个故事。

这是阿那托尔·法朗士讲的，这位现存的最伟大的法国文人，在一本名叫《圣克莱尔之罪》的迷人的书里提到，一个圣僧有一天问魔鬼的精灵他对真理有什么看法。魔鬼回答说："真理是白的。"圣僧非常高兴，因为魔鬼也说真理是洁白的。可是魔鬼笑了并接着说:"我说真理是白的,但并没有说真理是纯洁无瑕的。你却以为白的意思就是纯洁无瑕,完美无缺。现在我可以使你看到,它绝不代表这些。"

于是魔鬼在僧人面前拿出一个大圆盘来,在上面画着成千的画像,有各种各样的颜色。每一个画像代表着一种宗教或一种哲学;并且都举着一面小旗,旗上各有题字。一个写道,"神只有一个";另一个写道,"神有几百万个";再一个宣称,"人类是不朽的";还有的则宣称,"只有神是不朽的"。所有这些题字,以最奇怪的方式,一个一个互相矛盾着。正当僧人对这一景象感到惊奇的时候,魔鬼忽然把盘子转动起来——越转越快,直到声如雷鸣。立刻,各种颜色都不见了,盘子白得和月光一样;于是魔鬼笑着说:"这就是真理——你看它是白的。"

商君書

选译

来,满上一杯,就着春天的骄阳,
抛掉你悔恨的冬裳。
时间这鸟儿不会飞得太远,
而它啊已开始展翅飞翔。

不管是在乃沙堡或者巴比伦，
也不管杯中酒是苦涩还是芳醇，
生命的酒在一滴滴地流淌，
生命之树的叶子正一片一片凋落飞纷。

人们倾心于尘世的希望,
有的成功了,有的只好埋葬,
像沙漠的白雪,皑皑
一两个小时 —— 就不知去向。

试想,这是个破旧的客栈,
它的大门是交替的白天和夜晚;
那一个个扬威耀武的苏丹,
他的日子待够了,就一去不返。

有的人整天在思考信仰和教义，
有的人在考虑是肯定还是怀疑；
从暗处忽然有一个声音传来，
"愚人啊，这里和那里都没有真谛。"

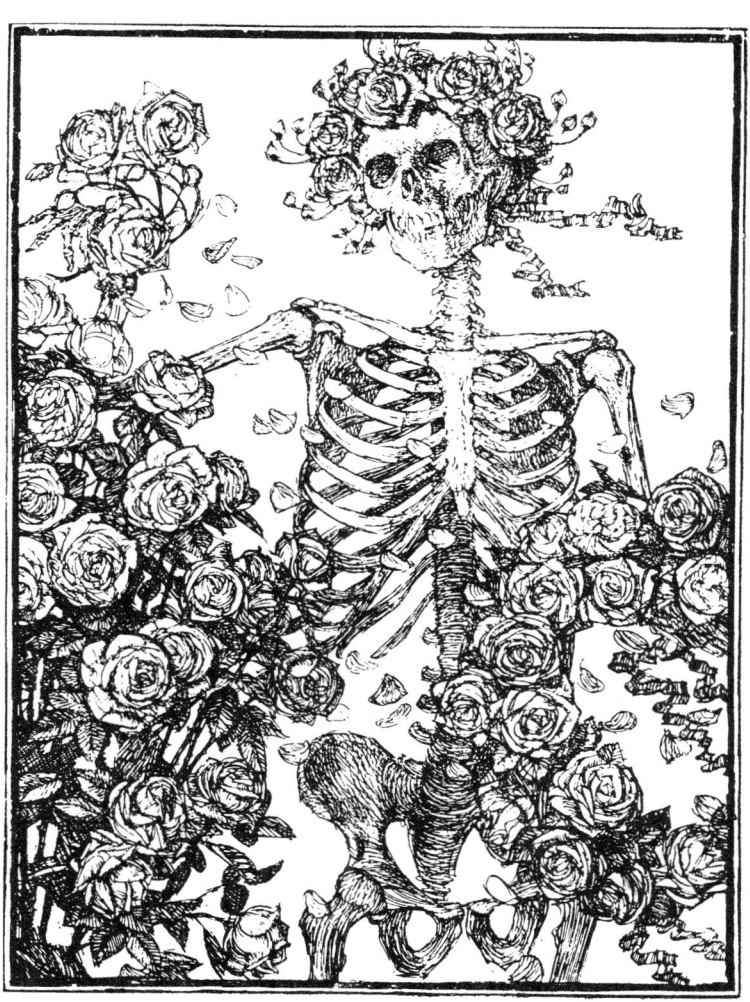

所有圣哲和智者关于两个世界的谈话，
不管它们是怎样的浩瀚无涯，
都不过是愚蠢的预言。他们的话
一钱不值，他们的嘴也塞满了泥巴。

当我年青的时候，我曾带着渴望去访问
博士和圣人，听那些伟大的高论
说天堂和地狱是这样或者那样，
而每次出来时却还是当初我进去的门。

我们一起播智慧的种，
我还亲手让它生长茏葱；
可是我只有这点儿收获啊——
我是来如流水去如风。

不知道是为了什么,来到这宇宙中间,
不知道从何而来,像流水潺潺,
离开这世界,像沙漠里的风,
呜呜地吹着,也不知去向哪边。

我靠拢这可怜的土罐的口外
想听听生命的奥秘何在；
嘴对着嘴,它说,"趁你活着时,
喝吧！—— 因为,一死了,你再不会回来。"

我想这轻声回答的罐儿,也曾经
一度是活着的人,他也会开怀畅饮,
唉! 和我接触的这罐口啊
也曾接受过并给过别人多少次爱吻!

因为我记得我曾停留在一个路旁，
看见制陶人在拍打他湿润的土样；
这陶土用它已经不在的舌头说，"兄弟，
我也曾是和你一样的人，请你轻拿轻放！"

不要为天上人间的事陷入迷惘，
明日的麻烦最好是让它随风飘扬；
且把你的手指插入她的卷发，
莫辜负那苗条女郎的劝酒持觞。

这帐篷只是供他一夜的休歇,
苏丹啊也正被带往死亡的陵穴;
苏丹起床了,侍者铺平床单,
准备迎送另一位过客。

不要怕有一天**生存**会合起你我的账本，
从此后一切就荡然无存；
那永生的**斟酒人**会从他的酒瓶里倒出
成百万我们这样的酒花，并不断酌斟。

当你和我消失在幕后的时候，
这世界还将长久长久地存留，
它看待我们的来去，
正像大海里投入一片小小的石头。

他的神秘的存在,在造物的川流中
像水银一样流动,使你徒劳追踪,
他会化作各样的形体,如鱼似月,
这也都将改变和死亡 —— 而**他**却无始无终。

好像被猜到了 —— 却又在帷幕后边,
围浸在黑暗中的戏还在上演,
这只是为了给**永恒**消遣
他自己编剧,自己导演,又自己看。

拿卑污的泥土造人是你的决策，
在乐园里又安置了那一条蛇；
对一切使人类颜面无光的罪过
要请**你**原恕——也请**你**负责！

哦,对地狱的恐惧,对天堂的希望!
至少一件事还是真的 —— 此生正在飞翔,
只有这件事是真的,其他都是说谎;
曾经开放的花儿已永远凋亡。

这岂不奇怪？成千上万的人
在我们之前走进了那黑暗的门，
却没有一个回来告诉我们，
哪里是我们要去的途程。

圣徒和学者给过我们很多的教导，
他们生在我们之前，已被当作先知埋掉，
都不过是一些梦话，是他们从睡梦中醒来
告诉旁人的，跟着又睡他们的长觉。

我叫我的灵魂去那虚无之乡，
对身后的情况进行探访；
慢慢地他又回到我的身边，
回复说："我自己就是地狱，也是天堂。"

天堂不过是欲望得到满足的幻景,
地狱是一个煎熬中灵魂的暗影,
投身在这黑暗之中,从那里我们
出来是如此之晚,而归去又过早地凋零。

我们不过是这样的一群
像走马灯似的往来的阴影,
围着太阳点着的灯笼在转,
半夜里高举这灯笼的是剧场的**主人**。

在这白天和黑夜交织的棋盘里,
他拿这些无能为力的棋子游戏,
把他们这里那里挪动,又将军,又杀子,
最后啊一个个放回棋盒里歇息。

球啊,它无法问明这样或者那样
而是由击球者打向左方右方;
只有将你投入球场的**他**
才知道这一切
　　　　　—— **他**才知详 —— **他**才知详!

那动着的手指在写,写过了又写下去,
不管你有多么聪明,有怎样虔诚的情绪,
都不会唤回**他**删去半行,
所有你的泪水也不会洗掉它一字一句。

唉！那随着玫瑰凋谢而逝去的春光！
那中断了的青春而芬芳的篇章！
那在树枝中歌唱的夜莺，
谁知道是来自又去向何方！

那边又升起了照着我们的明月 ——
今后啊她还会不断地圆缺，
今后啊她还会升起来寻找我们，
但在这花园里 —— 有一人将遍寻不得。

啊，女郎，几时你和她一样
在那草地上群星般的宾客中来往，
请你斟酒时把满满一杯美酒
倾洒在我曾经坐过的地方！

以上根据 Fitzgerald 版本选译
以下根据 Whinfield 版本选译

在这世界上我们只有一日的逗留，
我们得到的也只是不幸和烦愁，
留下了不解之谜和满怀遗憾，
然后，勉强踏上那黑暗的征途。

不管你做什么,不要伤你兄弟的心,
也不要让怒火搅扰别人的安宁;
假如你想得到永恒的幸福,
只使你自己烦恼,不要去烦恼别人。

严肃让人们没有一点快感,
沉醉又叫我神志昏颠;
这里有我的一个中庸之道,
既不完全醉倒,又不过分庄严。

在教堂、庙宇、清真寺和学校里边，
讲的不是地狱的恐怖就是天国的乐园，
但是真正懂得**安拉**奥秘的人们，
从来不把这些瘪谷播向人们的心田。

我梦见一位智者在说:"为什么让睡眠
把生命消磨?睡眠怎能开出幸福的花朵?
不要老去找死亡的孪生兄弟,
在坟墓里你有的是睡觉的时间!"

假如你懂得人世间生命的秘密,
死亡时我敢说你也就会了解神秘的**上帝**,
但如果,在你活着时,还什么也不知道,
那么,明天,你自己都不在了,又何从知悉?

现在你的玫瑰正开着幸福的花朵,
拿起你的酒杯来莫轻易错过,
及时行乐吧!时间是一个骗子,
像这样的日子你不会有多。

海亚姆,他曾长期编织过学术的网,
现在他是焚烧着,他已被送进了炉膛,
死神的剪刀剪断了他生命的线,
命运的掮客轻蔑地卖掉他,毫不心伤。

在世上谁要跟着欲求的脚印走路，
在你离去时将是一个穷人，也无人相助，
常常想想你是谁，是从哪里来的，
你在干什么，哪里又是你的归宿。

在死神的箭下没有可靠的盾牌，
世上的荣华富贵都将化作尘埃，
环顾这世界，我看不到一样好的东西，
除了善，一切都不值得人爱。

当**安拉**拌和我的泥土之时,我的整个生涯
他早就安排定了,件件事**他**都能预告无差;
没有**他**的旨意,我什么也做不出来,
这难道就是为了让我去地狱接受惩罚?

要提防命运夫人狡诈的微笑！
要当心她那锋利无比的弯刀！
假如她送一块香甜的肉到你口里，
那是有毒的 —— 千万莫把它吞掉！

黄金不能生出智慧,但智慧缺少面包
会使大地的花毡像一座地牢;
是荷包满满的玫瑰才会微笑,
空着手的紫罗兰只好是垂首无聊。

命运的车轮曾使多少人哭泣号啕,
它也吹落了许多玫瑰的花苞;
不要自以为年轻力壮,
有多少花芽还未开放就已枯焦。

对一个真诚的爱人,美和丑有什么关系?
不管她是穿着麻袋还是绸衣,
不管她是埋在地下,或是升上了天,
是呀,哪怕她下了地狱,他也要追到身边。

以前啊,在壮年的自负消逝之前,
我以为所有生命问题的答案我都已了然;
现在年纪大了也聪明了一点,才知道
我的生命虚度了,一切都是空谈,但为时已晚。

当海亚姆的名字和名誉消失之后
这世界还要长留,
以前没有我们,也无人注意,
在我们死后,一切又依然照旧。

智者们勘测了海洋和大地，
想寻找和了解它们的秘密——
我心里却感到十分怀疑
他们可会弄得清这宇宙的设计？

在你的灵魂里要十分小心,
对世上的事情要少加评论;
就好像你又聋又哑又看不见,可是你
照样有你的耳朵、你的舌头和你的眼睛。

让他去享受他那块面包,
和能够安睡的小巢,
不是别人的奴隶,也不要去奴役别人,
—— 说真的,这就是一代天骄。

让我的手总不和酒杯分开，
我的心总倾注着对一位美丽女郎的爱！
他们说："请**安拉**帮助你忏悔吧！"
就是有**安拉**的帮助，我仍然忏悔不来。

喝酒尽管不对,请注意同你喝酒的对手,
喝酒的你是谁,你又喝的是什么酒;
只要注意了这些,你就放胆地喝吧,
这样不是最聪明的人谁还能喝酒!

追求幸福的意识告诉我们，
抓住当前的快乐，放下眼前的忧心；
她说，我们不会像牧场上的草，
割去了，还会重生。

上天日日都增添我们的忧愁，
也从不说哪样快乐他不会带走；
假如未生之人知道我们的灾难，
请你想吧，他们是来还是留？

为什么老抱着未来痴想
并为些无谓的烦恼神伤?
别操心,把**安拉**的计划还给他,
他做计划时也没有和你商量。

所有逝去的人而今安在，
谁回来讲过他们去到的世界？
应做的事情及时做完，
因为你去了，再不会回来。

对聪明而可敬的人你可以寄托你的生命,
对那些毫无价值的人最好是远离一程;
敢从智者的手里拿来毒药,
愚人就给你灵丹妙药也不要沾唇。

这是一个用深刻的智慧制作的圣杯，
这标志着造物主看待它如何宝贵；
可是宇宙的**制陶人**却拿起他的杰作，
在地上把它摔得粉碎！

我多恼火你哟，命运的转轮！
让我从你的铁链下脱身！
假如只有愚人能得到你的照顾，
那就照顾我一下 —— 因为我也不太聪明。

我曾经徒劳地和贪欲进行斗争，
想到我丑恶的行为就觉得羞耻伤心；
我相信**你**会饶恕我的罪过，
就是这样啊,羞愧依然长存。

我们在世上不会久留,但现时在这里
抛弃了酒和爱岂不是愚蠢无比?
管它这世界是永久或只是暂存,
反正你是要走的,这和你有什么关系?

一手捧着《古兰经》,一手又把酒杯干,
我一半是错误,一半也不尽然;
那像蓝色大理石的天望着我,
"一个遗憾的穆斯林,倒也还不完全异端。"

我自己越不存在，我越生活得久长，
我越自卑下，越感到自己在高翔；
奇怪呀！我越是多喝这**生命**的酒，
就越发明智，也越发端庄。

充分了解这世界情况的人，
对人世的祸福都一视同仁，
因为不论遭遇的是祸还是福，
福无常往，祸也有它一定的时辰。

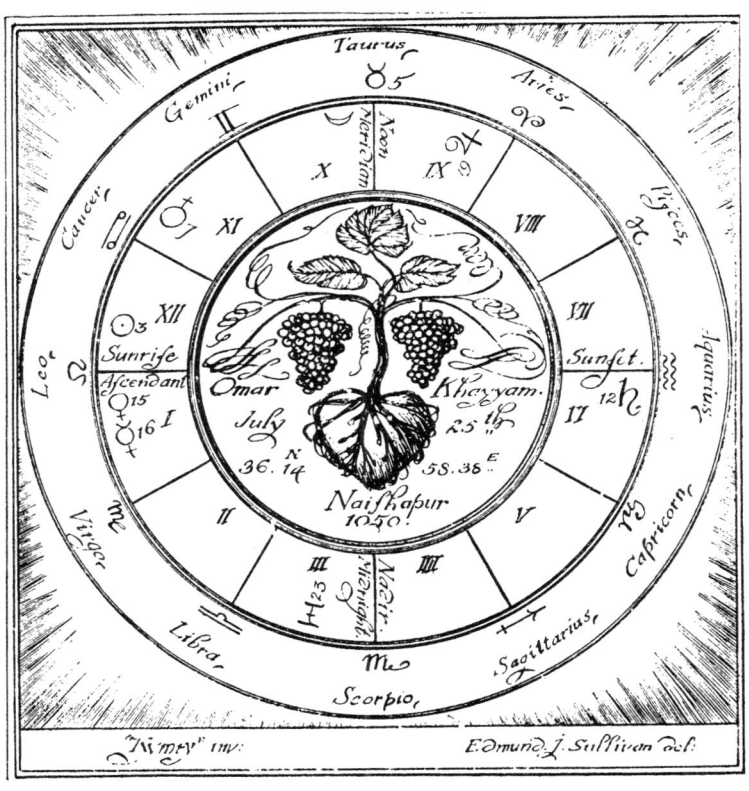

不要叹息幸福不能常在，
起来，抓住她眼前的宠爱；
假如，幸福永远只忠于一人，
那么什么时候好运才轮到你来？

不要想猜透那黑暗之**谜**,我的心!
多少聪明人都失败了,难道你能完成?
喝一杯吧,让这里就是你的天堂,
谁知道上边天堂里有没有你的份?

智慧的指示中有两条最关重要，
比你知道的传统的知识都高；
宁可吃斋不要吃不管什么样的肉，
和一切人都做朋友还不如孤独。

哦,我爱,在你办得到的时候,
用你的纤手扫去你爱人心上的忧愁;
你的优雅和美丽都不会长久,
它们将从你身上溜走,一去不留!

振作吧,现在你还没喝到死神的酒,
无情的命运也没有下你的毒手;
在这里做出点什么吧,对空着手
前去的人,那里一样也没有!

一个教主对一个妓女说：
"你好像是狂饮和淫乱的奴隶。"
她回答说："我正是这个样儿，
但先生，你是否表里如一？"

让一个人快乐和高兴，
远胜于在沙漠里有一群人；
让爱情的链子拴住一个自由者，
胜过把一千俘虏放出囚城。

只要你有四两酒，
你就喝掉它，像一个酒徒；
谁这样，谁就将精神朗爽，
不像你装模作样，也不像我这样忧愁。

他们一定说你坏,只要你有了名,
你要独自生活,他们又说你阴险深沉;
相信我,就算你是恺撒或者先知伊利亚,
也最好是不认识谁,并且也无人知闻。

从精神世界上我得到这一秘密,
人啊,造物把一切都集中于你;
是天使,是魔鬼,是人也是禽兽,
是呀,就看你在怎样表现自己!

译 后 记

　　对诗人的最好的介绍当然是他自己的诗,但一个高明评论家的解说有时也是引人入胜的,所以就以小泉八云的文章代序了。

　　奥玛的诗,从一出世就是有争论的,见仁见智,各有不同,大概到今天也还会这样;然而一边争论着,一边传诵着,又是光明磊落的文字,其中大概会不无道理吧。这里我只想指出一点:或许由于奥玛同时是一位天文学家和数学家的缘故,他的诗是不乏哲理的,这不多的译作中,就有诗人的宇宙观和他对于真理与信仰、人生的意义、生命的飘忽、命运的渺茫的思索。虽然他的结论倾向于对这些永恒的问题,谁也不能给出令人信服的答案,你最好是抓住即将从你手中消失的现实,正当地享受生活,趁你活着时能有所贡献,不做别人的奴隶,也不去奴役别人。这些小诗在读者心中将引起什么样的共鸣,却是很难说的,但可以肯定会因人而异,恐怕它能起的也只是一点催化作用而已。正如诗中所说:人本身"是天使,是魔鬼,是人也是禽兽",只看你如何表现。

  书中 Fitzgerald 的译文所据是 Louis Untermeyer 1947 年的汇编本 *Rubáiyát of Omar Khayyám* (Random House)。另一选本是 Whinfield, E. H. 1883 年同波斯文对照刊印的译本 *The Quatrains of Omar Khayyám*(Truber and Co.)。

  另外,和小泉八云一样,对有些典故多需要注释的诗,我很少试译,有些因难以传神协韵的也只好割爱。但这七十多首,已经足够概括奥玛诗的内容和风格,而不在乎其多少。四行诗的韵律好像中国的绝句,一、二、四行押韵。译时虽力求达旨和保持原诗的韵味,但由于译者笔拙,不免会略有出入或音节多少韵律不谐,则留待通家的修订和指正。

       一九八六年清明 鹤西 记

RUBÁIYÁT
OF
OMAR KHAYYÁM

RENDERED INTO ENGLISH VERSE BY
Edward Fitzgerald

FIFTH VERSION

OMAR KHAYYÁM,

THE ASTRONOMER-POET OF PERSIA.

OMAR KHAYYÁM was born at Naishápúr in Khorassán in the latter half of our Eleventh, and died within the First Quarter of our Twelfth Century. The Slender Story of his Life is curiously twined about that of two other very considerable Figures in their Time and Country: one of whom tells the Story of all Three. This was Nizám ul Mulk, Vizier to Alp Arslan the Son, and Malik Shah the Grandson, of Toghrul Beg the Tartar, who had wrested Persia from the feeble Successor of Mahmúd the Great, and founded that Seljukian Dynasty which finally roused Europe into the Crusades. This Nizám ul Mulk, in his *Wasiyat* —— or

Testament —— which he wrote and left as a Memorial for future Statesmen —— relates the following, as quoted in the *Calcutta Review*, No. 59, from Mirkhond's History of the Assassins.

"'One of the greatest of the wise men of Khorassán was the Imám Mowaffak of Naishápúr, a man highly honored and reverenced, —— may God rejoice his soul; his illustrious years exceeded eighty-five, and it was the universal belief that every boy who read the Korán or studied the traditions in his presence, would assuredly attain to honor and happiness. For this cause did my father send me from Tús to Naishápúr with Abd-us-samad, the doctor of law, that I might employ myself in study and learning under the guidance of that illustrious teacher. Towards me he ever turned an eye of favor and kindness, and as his pupil I felt for him extreme affection and devotion, so that I passed four years in his service. When I first came there, I found two other pupils of mine own age newly arrived, Hakim Omar Khayyám, and the ill-fated Ben Sabbáh. Both were endowed with sharpness of wit and the highest natural powers; and we three formed a close friendship together. When the Imám rose from his lectures, they used to join me, and we repeated to each other the lessons we had heard. Now Omar was a native of Naishápúr, while Hasan Ben Sabbáh's father was one Ali, a man of austere life and practise, but heretical in his creed and doctrine. One day Hasan said to me and to Khayyám, "It is a universal belief that the pupils of the Imám Mowaffak will attain to fortune. Now, even if we *all* do not attain thereto, without doubt one of us will; what then shall be our mutual pledge and bond?" We answered, "Be it what you please." "Well," he said, "let us make a vow, that to whomsoever this fortune falls, he shall share it equally with the rest, and reserve no pre-eminence for himself." "Be it so," we both replied, and on those terms we mutually pledged our words. Years rolled on, and I went from Khorassán to Transoxiana, and wandered to Ghazni and Cabul; and when I returned, I was invested with office, and rose to be administrator of affairs during the Sultanate of Sultán Alp Arslán.'

"He goes on to state, that years passed by, and both his old school-friends found him out, and came and claimed a share in his good fortune, according to the school-day vow. The Vizier was generous and kept his word. Hasan demanded a place in the government, which the Sultán granted at the Vizier's request; but discontented with a gradual rise, he plunged into the maze of intrigue of an oriental court, and, failing in a base attempt to supplant his benefactor, he was disgraced and fell. After many mishaps and wanderings, Hasan became the head of the Persian sect of the *Ismailians,* ——

a party of fanatics who had long murmured in obscurity, but rose to an evil eminence under the guidance of his strong and evil will. In A.D. 1090, he seized the castle of Alamút, in the province of Rúdbar, which lies in the mountainous tract south of the Caspian Sea; and it was from this mountain home he obtained that evil celebrity among the Crusaders as the OLD MAN OF THE MOUNTAINS, and spread terror through the Mohammedan world; and it is yet disputed whether the word *Assassin*, which they have left in the language of modern Europe as their dark memorial, is derived from the *hashish*, or opiate of hemp—leaves (the Indian *bhang*), with which they maddened themselves to the sullen pitch of oriental desperation, or from the name of the founder of the dynasty, whom we have seen in his quiet collegiate days, at Naishápúr. One of the countless victims of the Assassin's dagger was Nizám ul Mulk himself, the old school—boy friend.[1]

"Omar Khayyám also came to the Vizier to claim his share; but not to ask for title or office. 'The greatest boon you can confer on me,' he said, 'is to let me live in a corner under the shadow of your fortune, to spread wide the advantages of Science, and pray for your long life and prosperity.' The Vizier tells us, that when he found Omar was really sincere in his refusal, he pressed him no further, but granted him a yearly pension of

1200 *mithkáls* of gold from the treasury of Naishápúr.

"At Naishápúr thus lived and died Omar Khayyám, 'busied,' adds the Vizier, 'in winning knowledge of every kind, and especially in Astronomy, wherein he attained to a very high pre-eminence. Under the Sultanate of Malik Shah, he came to Merv, and obtained great praise for his proficiency in science, and the Sultán showered favors upon him.'

"When the Malik Shah determined to reform the calendar, Omar was one of the eight learned men employed to do it; the result was the *Jaláli* era (so called from *Jalál-ud-din*, one of the king's names) – 'a computation of time,' says Gibbon, 'which surpasses the Julian, and approaches the accuracy of the Gregorian style.' He is also the author of some astronomical tables, entitled 'Zíji-Malikshahí,' and the French have lately republished and translated an Arabic Treatise of his on Algebra.

"His Takhallus or poetical name (Khayyám) signifies a Tent-maker, and he is said to have at one time exercised that trade, perhaps before Nizám-ul-Mulk's generosity raised him to independence. Many Persian poets similarly derive their names from their occupations; thus we have Attár, 'a druggist,' Assár, 'an oil presser,' etc.[②] Omar himself alludes to his name in the following whimsical lines: ——

> "'Khayyám, who stitched the tents of science,
> Has fallen in grief's furnace and been suddenly burned;
> The shears of Fate have cut the tent ropes of his life,
> And the broker of Hope has sold him for nothing!'

"We have only one more anecdote to give of his Life, and that relates to the close; it is told in the anonymous preface which is sometimes prefixed to his poems; it has been printed in the Persian in the Appendix to Hyde's *Veterum Persarum Religio*, p. 499; and D'Herbelot alludes to it in his Bibliothèque, under *Khiam*.③ ——

"'It is written in the chronicles of the ancients that this King of the Wise, Omar Khayyám, died at Naishápúr in the year of the Hegira, 517 (A.D. 1123); in science he was unrivaled, —— the very paragon of his age. Khwájah Nizámi of Samarcand, who was one of his pupils, relates the following story: "I often used to hold conversations with my teacher, Omar Khayyám, in a garden; and one day he said to me, 'My tomb shall be in a spot where the north wind may scatter roses over it.' I wondered at the words he spake, but I knew that his were no idle words.④ Years after, when I chanced to revisit Naishápúr, I went to his final resting-place, and lo! it was just outside a garden, and trees laden with fruit stretched their boughs over the garden wall, and dropped their flowers upon his tomb, so that the stone was hidden under them."'"

Thus far —— without fear of Trespass —— from the *Calcutta Review*. The writer of it, on reading in India this story of Omar's Grave, was reminded, he says, of Cicero's Account of finding Archimedes' Tomb at Syra—cuse, buried in grass and weeds. I think Thorwaldsen desired to have roses grow over him; a wish religiously fulfilled for him to the present day, I believe. However, to return to Omar.

Though the Sultán "shower'd Favors upon him," Omar's Epicurean Audacity of Thought and Speech caused him to be regarded askance in his own Time and Country. He is said to have been especially hated and dreaded by the Súfis, whose Practise he ridiculed, and whose Faith amounts to little more than his own, when stript of the Mysticism and formal recognition of Is—lamism under which Omar would not hide. Their Poets, including Háfiz, who are (with the exception of Fir—dausi) the most considerable in Persia, borrowed largely, indeed, of Omar's material, but turning it to a mystical Use more convenient to Themselves and the People they addressed; a People quite as quick of Doubt as of Belief; as keen of Bodily sense as of Intellectual; and de—lighting in a cloudy composition of both, in which they could float luxuriously between Heaven and Earth, and this World and the Next, on the wings of a poetical

163

expression, that might serve indifferently for either. Omar was too honest of Heart as well of Head for this. Having failed (however mistakenly) of finding any Providence but Destiny, and any World but This, he set about making the most of it; preferring rather to soothe the Soul through the Senses into Acquiescence with Things as he saw them, than to perplex it with vain disquietude after what they *might* be. It has been seen, however, that his Worldly Ambition was not exorbitant; and he very likely takes a humorous or perverse pleasure in exalting the gratification of Sense above that of the Intellect, in which he must have taken great delight, although it failed to answer the Questions in which he, in common with all men, was most vitally interested.

For whatever Reason, however, Omar as before said, has never been popular in his own Country, and therefore has been but scantily transmitted abroad. The MSS. of his Poems, mutilated beyond the average Casualties of Oriental Transcription, are so rare in the East as scarce to have reacht Westward at all, in spite of all the acquisitions of Arms and Science. There is no copy at the India House, none at the Bibliothèque Nationale of Paris. We know but of one in England: No. 140 of the Ouseley MSS. at the Bodleian, written at Shiráz, A.D. 1460. This contains but 158 Rubáiyát. One in the Asiatic

Society's Library at Calcutta (of which we have a Copy), contains (and yet incomplete) 516, though swelled to that by all kinds of Repetition and Corruption. So Von Hammer speaks of *his* Copy as containing about 200, while Dr. Sprenger catalogues the Lucknow MS. at double that number. ⑤ The Scribes, too, of the Oxford and Calcutta MSS. seem to do their Work under a sort of Protest; each beginning with a Tetrastich (whether genuine or not), taken out of its alphabetical order; the Oxford with one of Apology; the Calcutta with one of Expostulation, supposed (says a Notice prefixed to the MS.) to have arisen from a Dream, in which Omar's mother asked about his future fate. It may be rendered thus:

> "Oh Thou who burn'st in Heart for those who burn
> In Hell, whose fires thyself shall feed in turn,
> How long be crying, 'Mercy on them, God!'
> Why, who art Thou to teach, and He to learn?"

The Bodleian Quatrain pleads Pantheism by way of Justification.

> "If I myself upon a looser Creed
> Have loosely strung the Jewel of Good deed,
> Let this one thing for my Atonement plead:
> That One for Two I never did misread."

The Reviewer,⑥ to whom I owe the Particulars of

Omar's Life, concludes his Review by comparing him with Lucretius, both as to natural Temper and Genius, and as acted upon by the Circumstances in which he lived. Both indeed were men of subtle, strong, and cultivated Intellect, fine Imagination, and Hearts passionate for Truth and Justice; who justly revolted from their Country's false Religion, and false, or foolish, Devotion to it; but who fell short of replacing what they subverted by such better *Hope* as others, with no better Revelation to guide them, had yet made a Law to themselves. Lucretius indeed, with such material as Epicurus furnished, satisfied himself with the theory of a vast machine fortuitously constructed, and acting by a Law that implied no Legislator; and so composing himself into a Stoical rather than Epicurean severity of Attitude, sat down to contemplate the mechanical drama of the Universe which he was part Actor in; himself and all about him (as in his own sublime description of the Roman Theater) discolored with the lurid reflex of the Curtain suspended between the Spectator and the Sun. Omar, more desperate, or more careless of any so complicated System as resulted in nothing but hopeless Necessity, flung his own Genius and Learning with a bitter or humorous jest into the general Ruin which their insufficient glimpses only served to reveal; and, pretending sensual pleasure, as the serious purpose of

Life, only *diverted* himself with speculative problems of Deity, Destiny, Matter and Spirit, Good and Evil, and other such questions, easier to start than to run down, and the pursuit of which becomes a very weary sport at last!

With regard to the present Translation. The original Rubáiyát (as, missing an Arabic Guttural, these *Tetrastichs* are more musically called) are independent Stanzas, consisting each of four Lines of equal, though varied, Prosody; sometimes *all* rhyming, but oftener (as here imitated) the third line a blank. Somewhat as in the Greek Alcaic, where the penultimate line seems to lift and suspend the Wave that falls over in the last. As usual with such kind of Oriental Verse, the Rubáiyát follow one another according to Alphabetic Rhyme ——— a strange succession of Grave and Gay. Those here selected are strung into something of an Eclogue, with perhaps a less than equal proportion of the "Drink and make-merry," which (genuine or not) recurs over-frequently in the Original. Either way, the Result is sad enough: saddest perhaps when most ostentatiously merry: more apt to move Sorrow than Anger toward the old Tent-maker, who, after vainly endeavoring to unshackle his Steps from Destiny, and to catch some authentic Glimpse of TO-MORROW, fell back upon TO-DAY (which has outlasted so many TO-MORROWS!) as the

only Ground he had got to stand upon, however mo‐
mentarily slipping from under his Feet.

EDWARD J. FITZGERALD

① Some of Omar's Rubáiyát warn us of the danger of Greatness, the instability of Fortune, and while advocating Charity to all Men, recom‐mending us to be too intimate with none. Attár makes Nizám‐ul‐Mulk use the very words of his friend Omar [Rub. xxviii.], "When Nizám‐ul‐Mulk was in the Agony (of Death) he said, 'Oh God! I am passing away in the hand of the wind.'"

② Though all these, like our Smiths, Archers, Millers, Fletchers, etc., may simply retain the Surname of an hereditary calling.

③ "Philosophe Musulman qui a vécu en Odeur de Sainteté dans sa Religion, vers la Fin du premier et le Commencement du second Siècle," no part of which, except the "Philosophe," can apply to our Khayyám.

④ The Rashness of the Words, according to D'Herbelot, consisted in being so opposed to those in the Korán: "No Man knows where he shall die." —— This story of Omar reminds me of another so naturally —— and when one remembers how wide of his humble mark the noble sailor aimed —— so pathetically told by Captain Cook —— not by Doctor Hawksworth —— in his Second Voyage (i. 374). When leaving Ulietea, "Oreo's last request was for me to return. When he saw he could not obtain that promise, he asked the name of my *Marai* (burying-place). As strange a question as this was, I hesitated not a moment to tell him 'Stepney'; the parish in which I live when in London. I was made to repeat it several times over till they could pronounce it; and then 'Stepney Marai no Toote' was echoed through a hundred mouths at once. I afterwards found the same question had been put to Mr. Forster by a man on shore; but he gave a different, and indeed more proper answer, by saying, 'No man who used the sea could say where he should be buried.'"

⑤ "Since this paper was written" (adds the Reviewer in a note), "we have met with a Copy of a very rare Edition, printed at Calcutta in 1836. This contains 438 Tetrastichs, with an Appendix containing 54 others not found in some MSS."

⑥ Professor Cowell.

RUBÁIYÁT OF OMAR KHAYYÁM

(Fifth Version)

I

WAKE! For the Sun, who scatter'd into flight
The Stars before him from the Field of Night,
    Drives Night along with them from Heav'n, and strikes
The Sultán's Turret with a Shaft of Light.

II

Before the phantom of False morning died,
Methought a Voice within the Tavern cried,
    "When all the Temple is prepared within,
Why nods the drowsy Worshiper outside?"

III

And, as the Cock crew, those who stood before
The Tavern shouted ——"Open then the Door!
    You know how little while we have to stay,
And, once departed, may return no more."

IV

Now the New Year reviving old Desires,
The thoughtful Soul to Solitude retires,
　Where the WHITE HAND OF MOSES on the Bough
Puts out, and Jesus from the Ground suspires.

V

Iram indeed is gone with all his Rose,
And Jamshyd's Sev'n—ring'd Cup where no one knows;
　But still a Ruby kindles in the Vine,
And many a Garden by the Water blows.

VI

And David's lips are lockt; but in divine
High—piping Péhlevi, with "Wine! Wine! Wine!
　Red Wine! " —— the Nightingale cries to the Rose
That sallow cheek of hers to' incarnadine.

VII

Come, fill the Cup, and in the fire of Spring
Your Winter garment of Repentance fling:
　The Bird of Time has but a little way
To flutter —— and the Bird is on the Wing.

VIII

Whether at Naishápúr or Babylon,
Whether the Cup with sweet or bitter run,
  The Wine of Life keeps oozing drop by drop,
The Leaves of Life keep falling one by one.

IX

Each Morn a thousand Roses brings, you say:
Yes, but where leaves the Roses of Yesterday?
  And this first Summer month that brings the Rose
Shall take Jamshyd and Kaikobád away.

X

Well, let it take them! What have we to do
With Kaikobád the Great, or Kaikhosrú?
  Let Zál and Rustum bluster as they will,
Or Hátim call to Supper —— heed not you.

XI

With me along the strip of Herbage strown
That just divides the desert from the sown,
  Where name of Slave and Sultán is forgot ——
And Peace to Mahmúd on his golden Throne!

XII

A Book of Verses underneath the Bough,
A Jug of Wine, a Loaf of Bread —— and Thou
   Beside me singing in the Wilderness ——
Oh, Wilderness were Paradise enow!

XIII

Some for the Glories of This World; and some
Sigh for the Prophet's Paradise to come;
   Ah, take the Cash, and let the Credit go,
 Nor heed the rumble of a distant Drum!

XIV

Look to the blowing Rose about us —— "Lo,
Laughing," she says, "into the world I blow,
   At once the silken tassel of my Purse
Tear, and its Treasure on the Garden throw."

XV

And those who husbanded the Golden grain,
And those who flung it to the winds like Rain,
   Alike to no such aureate Earth are turn'd
As, buried once, Men want dug up again.

XVI

The Worldly Hope men set their Hearts upon
Turns Ashes —— or it prospers; and anon,
   Like Snow upon the Desert's dusty Face,
Lighting a little hour or two —— is gone.

XVII

Think, in this batter'd Caravanserai
Whose Portals are alternate Night and Day,
   How Sultán after Sultán with his Pomp
Abode his destined Hour, and went his way.

XVIII

They say the Lion and the Lizard keep
The courts where Jamshyd gloried and drank deep:
   And Bahrám, that great Hunter —— the Wild Ass
Stamps o'er his Head, but cannot break his Sleep.

XIX

I sometimes think that never blows so red
The Rose as where some buried Cæsar bled;
   That every Hyacinth the Garden wears
Dropt in her Lap from some once lovely Head.

XX

And this reviving Herb whose tender Green
Fledges the River–Lip on which we lean ——
   Ah, lean upon it lightly! for who knows
From what once lovely Lip it springs unseen!

XXI

Ah, my Belovéd, fill the Cup that clears
TO-DAY of past Regrets and future Fears:
   To–morrow —— Why, To–morrow I may be
Myself with Yesterday's Sev'n thousand Years.

XXII

For some we loved, the loveliest and the best
That from his Vintage rolling Time hath prest,
   Have drunk their Cup a Round or two before,
And one by one crept silently to rest.

XXIII

And we, that now make merry in the Room
They left, and Summer dresses in new bloom,
   Ourselves must we beneath the Couch of Earth
Descend —— ourselves to make a Couch —— for whom?

XXIV

Ah, make the most of what we yet may spend,
Before we too into the Dust descend;
   Dust into Dust, and under Dust to lie,
Sans Wine, sans Song, sans Singer, and —— sans End!

XXV

Alike for those who for TO-DAY prepare,
And those that after some TO-MORROW stare,
   A Muezzín from the Tower of Darkness cries,
"Fools! your Reward is neither Here nor There."

XXVI

Why, all the Saints and Sages who discuss'd
Of the Two Worlds so wisely —— they are thrust
   Like foolish Prophets forth; their Words to Scorn
Are scatter'd, and their Mouths are stopt with Dust.

XXVII

Myself when young did eagerly frequent
Doctor and Saint, and heard great argument
   About it and about: but evermore
Came out by the same door where in I went.

XXVIII

With them the seed of Wisdom did I sow,
And with mine own hand wrought to make it grow;
   And this was all the Harvest that I reap'd ——
"I came like Water, and like Wind I go."

XXIX

Into this Universe, and *Why* not knowing
Nor *Whence*, like Water willy-nilly flowing;
   And out of it, as Wind along the Waste,
I know not *Whither*, willy-nilly blowing.

XXX

What, without asking, hither hurried *Whence*?
And, without asking, *Whither* hurried hence!
   Oh, many a Cup of this forbidden Wine
Must drown the memory of that insolence!

XXXI

Up from Earth's Center through the Seventh Gate
I rose, and on the Throne of Saturn sate,
   And many a Kont unravel'd by the Road;
But not the Master-knot of Human Fate.

XXXII

There was the Door to which I found no Key;
There was the Veil through which I might not see:
  Some little talk awhile of M<small>E</small> and T<small>HEE</small>
There was —— and then no more of T<small>HEE</small> and M<small>E</small>.

XXXIII

Earth could not answer; nor the Seas that mourn
In flowing Purple, of their Lord Forlorn;
  Nor rolling Heaven, with all his Signs reveal'd
And hidden by the sleeve of Night and Morn.

XXXIV

Then of the T<small>HEE IN</small> M<small>E</small> who works behind
The Veil, I lifted up my hands to find
  A lamp amid the Darkness; and I heard,
As from Without —— "T<small>HE</small> M<small>E WITHIN</small> T<small>HEE BLIND</small>! "

XXXV

Then to the Lip of this poor earthen Urn
I lean'd, the Secret of my Life to learn:
  And Lip to Lip it murmur'd —— "While you live,
Drink! —— for, once dead, you never shall return."

XXXVI

I think the Vessel, that with fugitive
Articulation answer'd, once did live,
    And drink; and Ah! the passive Lip I kiss'd,
    How many Kisses might it take —— and give!

XXXVII

For I remember stopping by the way
To watch a Potter thumping his wet Clay:
    And with its all—obliterated Tongue
    It murmur'd —— "Gently, Brother, gently, pray! "

XXXVIII

And has not such a Story from of Old
Down Man's successive generations roll'd
    Of such a clod of saturated Earth
Cast by the Maker into Human mold?

XXXIX

And not a drop that from our Cups we throw
For Earth to drink of, but may steal below
    To quench the fire of Anguish in some Eye
There hidden —— far beneath, and long ago.

XL

As then the Tulip for her morning sup
Of Heav'nly Vintage from the soil looks up,
   Do you devoutly do the like, till Heav'n
To Earth invert you —— like an empty Cup.

XLI

Perplext no more with Human or Divine,
To—morrow's tangle to the winds resign,
   And lose your fingers in the tresses of
The Cypress—slender Minister of Wine.

XLII

And if the Wine you drink, the Lip you press,
End in what All begins and ends in —— Yes;
   Think then you are TO-DAY what YESTERDAY
You were —— TO-MORROW you shall not be less.

XLIII

So when that Angel of the darker Drink
At last shall find you by the river—brink,
   And, offering his Cup, invite your Soul
Forth to your Lips to quaff —— you shall not shrink.

XLIV

Why, if the Soul can fling the Dust aside,
And naked on the Air of Heaven ride,
    Were't not a Shame —— were't not a Shame for him
In this clay carcass crippled to abide?

XLV

'Tis but a Tent where takes his one day's rest
A Sultán to the realm of Death addrest;
    The Sultán rises, and the dark Ferrash
Strikes, and prepares it for another Guest.

XLVI

And fear not lest Existence closing *your*
Account, and mine, should know the like no more;
    The Eternal Sákí from that Bowl has pour'd
Millions of Bubbles like us, and will pour.

XLVII

When You and I behind the Veil are past,
Oh, but the long, long while the World shall last,
    Which of our Coming and Departure heeds
As the Sea's self should heed a pebble-cast.

XLVIII

A Moment's Halt —— a momentary taste
Of BEING from the Well amid the Waste ——
    And Lo! —— the phantom Caravan has reach'd
The NOTHING it set out from —— Oh, make haste!

XLIX

Would you that spangle of Existence spend
About THE SECRET —— quick about it, Friend!
    A Hair perhaps divides the False from True ——
And upon what, prithee, may life depend?

L

A Hair perhaps divides the False and True;
Yes; and a single Alif were the clue ——
    Could you but find it —— to the Treasure—house,
And peradventuer to THE MASTER too;

LI

Whose secret Presence through Creation's veins
Running Quicksilver—like eludes your pains;
    Taking all shapes from Máh to Máhi and
They change and perish all —— but He remains;

LII

A moment guessed —— then back behind the Fold
Immerst of Darkness round the Drama roll'd
   Which, for the Pastime of Eternity,
He doth Himself contrive, enact, behold.

LIII

But if in vain, down on the stubborn floor
Of Earth, and up to Heav'n's unopening Door,
   You gaze TO-DAY, while You are You —— how then
TO-MORROW, when You shall be You no more?

LIV

Waste not your Hour, nor in the vain pursuit
Of This and That endeavor and dispute;
   Better be jocund with the fruitful Grape
Than sadden after none, or bitter, Fruit.

LV

You know, my Friends, with what a brave Carouse
I made a Second Marriage in my house;
   Divorced old barren Reason from my Bed,
And took the Daughter of the Vine to Spouse.

LVI

For "Is" and "Is—not" though with Rule and Line
And 'Up-and-down" by Logic I define,
   Of all that one should care to fathom, I
Was never deep in anything but —— Wine.

LVII

Ah, by my Computations, People say,
Reduce the Year to better reckoning? —— Nay,
   'Twas only striking from the Calendar
Unborn To-morrow and dead Yesterday.

LVIII

And lately, by the Tavern Door agape,
Came shining through the Dusk an Angel Shape
   Bearing a Vessel on his Shoulder; and
He bid me taste of it; and 'twas —— the Grape!

LIX

The Grape that can with Logic absolute
The Two-and-Seventy jarring Sects confute:
   The sovereign Alchemist that in a trice
Life's leaden metal into Gold transmute;

LX.

The mighty Mahmúd, Allah—breathing Lord,
That all the misbelieving and black Horde
  Of Fears and Sorrows that infest the Soul
Scatters before him with his whirlwind Sword.

LXI

Why, be this Juice the growth of God, who dare
Blaspheme the twisted tendril as a Snare?
  A Blessing, we should use it, should we not?
And if a Curse —— why, then, Who set it there?

LXII

I must abjure the Balm of Life, I must,
Scared by some After—reckoning ta'en on trust,
  Or lured with Hope of some Diviner Drink,
To fill the Cup —— when crumbled into Dust!

LXIII

Of threats of Hell and Hopes of Paradise!
One thing at least is certain —— *This* Life flies;
  One thing is certain and the rest is Lies;
The Flower that once has blown for ever dies.

LXIV

Strange, is it not? that of the myriads who
Before us pass'd the door of Darkness through,
　Not one returns to tell us of the Road,
Which to discover we must travel too.

LXV

The Revelations of Devout and Learn'd
Who rose before us, and as Prophets burn'd,
　Are all but Stories, which, awoke from Sleep
They told their comrades, and to Sleep return'd.

LXVI

I sent my Soul through the Invisible,
Some letter of that After—life to spell:
　And by and by my Soul return'd to me,
And answer'd "I Myself am Heav'n and Hell."

LXVII

Heav'n but the Vision of fulfill'd Desire,
And Hell the Shadow from a Soul on fire,
　Cast on the Darkness into which Ourselves,
So late emerged from, shall so soon expire.

LXVIII

We are no other than a moving row
Of Magic Shadow—shapes that come and go
   Round with the Sun—illumined Lantern held
In Midnight by the Master of the Show;

LXIX

But helpless Pieces of the Game He plays
Upon this Chequer—board of Nights and Days;
   Hither and thither moves, and checks, and slays,
And one by one back in the Closet lays.

LXX

The Ball no question makes of Ayes and Noes,
But Here or There as strikes the Player goes;
   And He that toss'd you down into the Field,
He knows about it all —— HE knows —— HE knows!

LXXI

The Moving Finger writes; and, having writ,
Moves on: nor all your Piety nor Wit
   Shall lure it back to cancel half a Line,
Nor all your Tears wash out a Word of it.

LXXII

And that inverted Bowl they call the Sky,
Whereunder crawling coop'd we live and die,
  Lift not your hands to *It* for help —— for It
As impotently moves as you or I.

LXXIII

With Earth's first Clay They did the Last Man knead,
And there of the Last Harvest sow'd the Seed:
  And the first Morning of Creation wrote
What the Last Dawn of Reckoning shall read.

LXXIV

YESTERDAY *This* Day's Madness did prepare;
TO-MORROW'S Silence, Triumph, or Despair:
  Drink! for you not know whence you came, nor why:
Drink! for you know not why you go nor where.

LXXV

I tell you this —— When, started from the Goal,
Over the flaming shoulders of the Foal
  Of Heav'n Parwín and Mushtarí they flung,
In my predestined Plot of Dust and Soul.

LXXVI

The Vine had struck a fibre: which about
If clings my Being —— let the Dervish flout;
    Of my Base metal may be filed a Key
That shall unlock the Door he howls without.

LXXVII

And this I know: whether the one True Light
Kindle to Love, or Wrath—consume me quite,
    One Flash of It within the Tavern caught
Better than in the Temple lost outright.

LXXVIII

What! out of senseless Nothing to provoke
A conscious Something to resent the yoke
    Of unpermitted Pleasure, under pain
Of Everlasting Penalties, if broke!

LXXIX

What! from his helpless Creature be repaid
Pure Gold for what he lent him dross—allay'd ——
    Sue for a Debt he never did contract,
And cannot answer —— Oh the sorry trade!

LXXX

Oh Thou, who didst with pitfall and with gin
Beset the Road I was to wander in,
 Thou wilt not with Predestined Evil round
Enmesh, and then impute my Fall to Sin!

LXXXI

Oh Thou, who Man of baser Earth didst make,
And ev'n with Paradise devise the Snake:
 For all the Sin wherewith the Face of Man
Is blacken'd —— Man's forgiveness give —— and take!

*   *   *   *   *   *

LXXXII

As under cover of departing Day
Slunk hunger-stricken Ramazán away,
 Once more within the Potter's house alone
I stood, surrounded by the Shapes of Clay.

LXXXIII

Shapes of all Sorts and Sizes, great and small,
That stood along the floor and by the wall;
 And some loquacious Vessels were; and some
Listen'd perhaps, but never talk'd at all.

LXXXIV

Said one among them —— "Surely not in vain
My substance of the common Earth was ta'en
   And to this Figure molded, to be broke,
Or trampled back to shapeless Earth again."

LXXXV

Then said a Second —— "Ne'er a peevish Boy
Would break the Bowl from which he drank in joy;
   And He that with his hand the Vessel made
Will surely not in after Wrath destroy."

LXXXVI

After a momentary silence spake
Some Vessel of a more ungainly Make;
   "They sneer at me for leaning all awry:
What! did the Hand then of the Potter shake?"

LXXXVII

Whereat some one of the loquacious Lot ——
I think a Súfi pipkin —— waxing hot ——
   "All this of Pot and Potter —— Tell me then,
Who is the Potter, pray, and who the Pot?"

LXXXVIII

"Why," said another, "Some there are who tell
Of one who threatens he will toss to Hell
    The luckless Pots he marr'd in making —— Pish!
He's a Good Fellow, and 'twill all be well."

LXXXIX

"Well," murmured one, "Let whoso make or buy,
My Clay with long Oblivion is gone dry:
    But fill me with the old familiar Juice,
Methinks I might recover by and by."

XC

So while the Vessels one by one were speaking,
The little Moon look'd in that all were seeking:
    And then they jogg'd each other, "Brother! Brother!
Now for the Porter's shoulders' knot a-creaking!"

*   *   *   *   *   *

XCI

Ah, with the Grape my fading life provide,
And wash the Body whence the Life has died,
   And lay me, shrouded in the living Leaf,
By some not unfrequented Garden—side.

XCII

That ev'n buried Ashes such a snare
Of Vintage shall fling up into the Air
   As not a True—believer passing by
But shall be overtaken unaware.

XCIII

Indeed the Idols I have loved so long
Have done my credit in this World much wrong:
   Have drown'd my Glory in a shallow Cup,
And sold my reputation for a Song.

XCIV

Indeed, indeed, Repentance oft before
I swore —— but was I sober when I swore?
   And then and then came Spring, and Rose—in—hand
My thread—bare Penitence apieces tore.

XCV

And much as Wine has play'd the Infidel,
And robb'd me of my Robe of Honor —— Well,
  I wonder often what the Vintners buy
One half so precious as the stuff they sell.

XCVI

Yet Ah, that Spring should vanish with the Rose!
That Youth's sweet-scented manuscript should close!
  The Nightingale that in the branches sang,
Ah whence, and whither flown again, who knows!

XCVII

Would but the Desert of the Fountain yield
One glimpse —— if dimly, yet indeed, reveal'd,
  To which the fainting Traveler might spring,
As springs the trampled herbage of the field!

XCVIII

Would but some wingéd Angel ere too late
Arrest the yet unfolded Roll of Fate,
  And make the stern Recorder otherwise
Enregister, or quite obliterate!

XCIX

Ah Love! could you and I with Him conspire
To grasp this sorry Scheme of Things entire,
   Would not we shatter it to bits —— and then
Re—mold it nearer to the Heart's Desire!

      *   *   *   *   *   *

C

Yon rising Moon that looks for us again ——
How oft hereafter will she wax and wane;
   How oft hereafter rising look for us
Through this same Garden —— and for *one* in vain!

CI

And when like her, oh Sákí, you shall pass
Among the Guests Star—scatter'd on the Grass,
   And in your joyous errand reach the spot
Where I made One —— turn down an empty Glass!

TAMAM.

出版后记

程侃声先生（1908 — 1999 CE），笔名鹤西，是中国著名的水稻专家。先生为中国的水稻种植业做出的重大贡献，在行内非常知名。大多数人都不知道，程先生在上世纪二十年代是很有名的诗人。废名（冯文炳）写的《莫须有先生传》里头的"一见面就握手，不胜亲热之至"的小朋友，说的就是程侃声先生。

程先生二十多岁的时候，作为诗人、翻译家，不断有作品在《晨报诗刊》（徐志摩、闻一多主编）、《小说月报》（叶圣陶代郑振铎主编）等重要刊物上发表。其实早在先生中学毕业的时候,他就是用自己翻译的稿酬来支付上大学的学费的。1929年,先生发现自己的译作有被抄袭的迹象,在《华北日报》上表达了疑问。本来很简单的事情,却遭到了周樟寿护短的、指鹿为马的猛烈抨击。一时间人言嘈嘈,先生为此,也就退出了这个浑水泥潭。

先生后来专心从事水稻科学的研究工作。他偶尔也写些诗歌散文,不为发表,只是自己喜欢。先生自己最看重的,就是《鲁拜集》译稿,以及回忆废名的文章。可惜的是,看到过先生译的《鲁拜集》的人很少。我早年和先生往来书札,讨论最多的就是《鲁拜集》。这些我和先生之间的数十通书信,后来全在美国辗转搬家的时候遗失了,这更让我不安。一部好的作品不失传,最好的办法就是把它印出来。现在印出这个集子,正好作为对先生去世十周年的纪念。

《鲁拜集》中文译本很多。先生曾和我说,诗集想要译好,很重要的一条是不能全都译。其实先生是全部都译过的。因为语言的转换,有的译文他自己不够满意,宁可就不拿出来。程先生拿出来的译文,都是声音韵律与内容表达上自己满意的。

本书的第一部分,就是程先生的作品,内容包括先生从日语译出的小泉八云的文章(代序)、从英文译出的《鲁拜集》诗选以及译后记。

本书的第二部分,则是英文本《鲁拜集》(菲氏译本第五版)。

本书的插图作者是美国知名画家 Edward J. Sullivan。Sullivan 为本书绘制的铜版画插图在出版之初,有几幅因为铜板制作中腐蚀过甚导致细节模糊,已经无法补救。我们这次出版,对于这几幅有遗憾的插图也一仍其旧。

Lewis Eden
Oct. 10. 2004

图书在版编目（CIP）数据

鲁拜集 /（波斯）海亚姆著；（英）菲茨吉拉德英译；鹤西汉译. ——北京：北京联合出版公司，2014.5
ISBN 978-7-5502-3056-9

Ⅰ.①鲁… Ⅱ.①海…②菲…③鹤… Ⅲ.①诗集—伊朗—中世纪 Ⅳ.① I373.23

中国版本图书馆 CIP 数据核字（2014）第 100534 号

Copyright © 2014 POST WAVE PUBLISHING CONSULTING (Beijing) Co., Ltd.
All rights reserved.
本书版权归属于后浪出版咨询（北京）有限责任公司。

鲁拜集

著　　者：（波斯）海亚姆
英 译 者：（英）爱德华·菲茨吉拉德 等
中 译 者：鹤　西
选题策划：后浪出版公司
出版统筹：吴兴元
特约编辑：马春华
责任编辑：王　巍
封面设计：周伟伟
版面设计：王雨薇
营销推广：ONEBOOK
装帧制造：墨白空间

北京联合出版公司出版
（北京市西城区德外大街 83 号楼 9 层　100088）
北京嘉实印刷有限公司印刷　新华书店经销
字数 120 千字　720×1030 毫米　1/32　7 印张　插页 3
2015 年 1 月第 1 版　2015 年 1 月第 1 次印刷
ISBN 978-7-5502-3056-9
定价：32.00 元

后浪出版咨询（北京）有限公司常年法律顾问：北京大成律师事务所　周天晖 copyright@hinabook.com
未经许可，不得以任何方式复制或抄袭本书部分或全部内容
版权所有，侵权必究
本书若有质量问题，请与本公司图书销售中心联系调换。电话：010-64010019